I AM BIRCH

By Scott Kelley

Islandport Press
P.O. Box 10
Yarmouth, Maine 04096
books@islandportpress.com
www.islandportpress.com

ISBN: 978-1-944762-39-1
Library of Congress Control Number: 2017912566

Dean Lunt, Publisher
Book design by Teresa Lagrange
Printed in USA by Versa Press

For Bob Maxon, my first spirit guide,
and for Gail and Abbott, who guide me still.
—Scott Kelley

Everyone
calls me
BIRCH,

for I am a birch tree,
much like any other.

At least,
I was a tree
until Beaver came along.
As he gnawed through my bark
and brought me crashing down,
he was mumbling.

"COLD AND DARKNESS,"
I heard him say,
"COLD AND DARKNESS."

Now,
I am a
stump.

Porcupine came slowly by, as porcupines do.
He yawned.
Then he told me about a coming time of great
COLD AND DARKNESS.

Everyone in the forest was terrified, he said.
They were spending their days stocking up.
I asked Porcupine, "Who did you hear this from?"
Porcupine shrugged and yawned again.
He said he thought he heard it from Deer.

Then he shambled off in the direction from which he
had come.

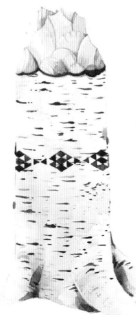

**Can I just say that porcupines
are utterly hopeless, of no use
to anyone, and be done with it?**

Deer came by.
I asked her if she was spreading word of
COLD AND DARKNESS.
"Not me," said Deer. "I heard it from Badger."

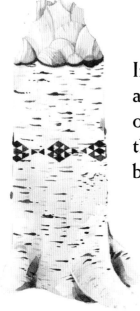

In fact, can I also say that deer
are simply too quiet for their
own good? So quiet, in fact, that
they startle not just each other,
but themselves, as well.

Badger came by, and I asked her if she was spreading word of

COLD AND DARKNESS.
"Not me," said Badger.
"I heard it from Heron."

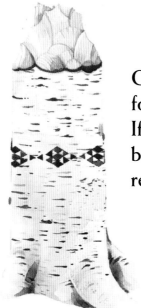

Can I now just praise badgers for being unbelievably tidy? If you are ever invited to a badger's home, definitely remember to wipe your feet.

Heron landed nearby, looking for fish,
and I yelled to him,
"Heron, have you been spreading word of
COLD AND DARKNESS?"

Heron looked at me in
that way herons have,
and flew away.

Squirrel came by and tripped over Rock,
who has been at the base of my trunk
for as long as I can remember.
"Hey!" said Rock. "Watch where you are going!"
Squirrel ran off, too fast to listen, her cheeks
full of nuts.

"Rock," I asked, "is it you who
has been spreading word of

COLD AND DARKNESS?"

"I am a rock," said Rock,
as if that explained everything.
"Right," I said. "You are a rock."

Squirrels.
If it's not a nut,
they just don't care.

Rabbit came by.
Just then, the shadow of Eagle darkened the ground.
Rabbit stopped dead still right in front of me.
"Rabbit," I asked,
"is it you who has been spreading word of

COLD AND DARKNESS?"

Rabbit said nothing, nose barely twitching.
He waited for the shadow of Eagle to move on,
then hopped off.

Typical Rabbit.

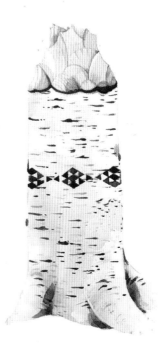

Moose and Bear came by, mouths full of blueberries.
"I heard the Cold is going to be very cold," Moose said.
"And I heard the Dark is going to be very dark," Bear replied.
"But the Cold is going to be colder than the Dark is going to be dark!"
"No, no . . . you've got it wrong: the Dark is going to be darker than the Cold is going to be cold!"

"Stop arguing," I said.
"Who told you about this very cold Cold
and this very dark Dark?"
"Can't remember," said Bear.
"Not sure, really," said Moose.

I saw the

CHAOS
OF FEAR

everywhere.

So many
trees cut
down,

blueberry
bushes
stripped
bare,

everyone running about.

Beaver came back, looking for more trees.
There were none.
"Beaver," I said, "are you the one who has been
spreading word of Cold and Darkness?"
"Yes!" said Beaver. He smiled. "I told everybody,
so they could prepare."
Beavers, you see, love to prepare.

"But who told you?" I asked.

"It was Rabbit. Or was it Deer?
No, wait, it was . . . oh, I don't know.
But they seemed quite sure!"

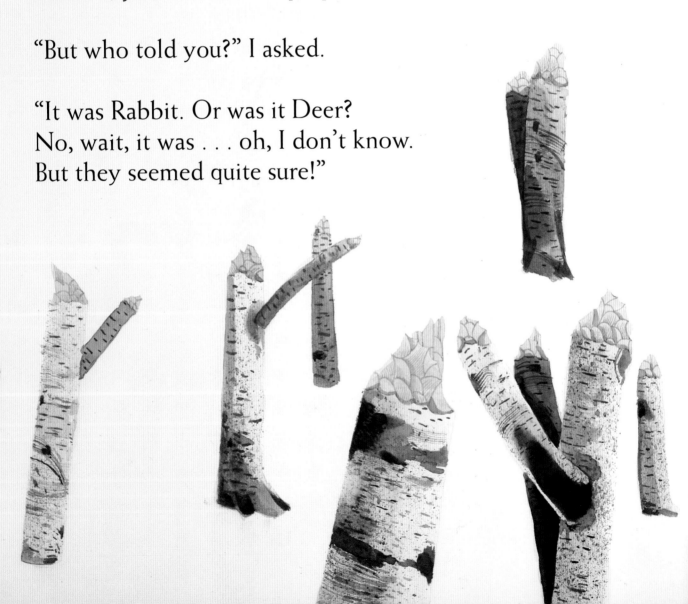

"There *is* no coming time of
great Cold and Darkness,"
I said.
"There never was."

Which, of course, was true. The foretold time of
Cold and Darkness never arrived. Beaver admitted his
mistake—which is hard for beavers—and spent days
wandering amongst the stumps, apologizing. He never
did remember where he had heard it. For all we know,
it could have been something the wind whispered,
on its way to somewhere else.

For a while, everyone talked about
Cold and Darkness, until they forgot.

Winds calmed, trees sprouted,
and the forest felt like home again.
Blueberries grew.

One day, an acorn fell before me.
"I will grow to be a mighty oak tree," Acorn said,
"but you will always be a stump."

Squirrel came by, picked up Acorn, and scurried off.
"Or maybe not," I called after Acorn.

Suddenly, a leaf sprung from one
of my remaining branches.
It sought the sun and the rain.
It worked very hard at being a leaf.

Over time—many, many years—
I grew into a huge, arching birch tree.

Animals gather here, though
none of them quite know why.

ABOUT THE BOOK

Stories of Gluskap—or Kluskap, Glooscap, or Gluskabe—have been passed down from generation to generation for hundreds of years by the native people of northern New England and Atlantic Canada. The Wabanaki—Micmac, Passamaquoddy, Penobscot, and Maliseet— tell various tales of him. He is a creator, a king, a cultural hero, a giant, or a legend. In some accounts, he is the creator of humans; in other accounts, he is sent by a creator or great spirit to help and teach humans. He is powerful, but makes mistakes and learns from them. In all the tales, Gluskap shows people how to exist in harmony with all living things.

The legends of Gluskap were part of artist Scott Kelley's childhood. One in particular, "How The Rabbit Got Long Ears," was a favorite. In it, Rabbit tells the other animals that the sun is not going to rise again, and Gluskap must set the record straight.

Kelley had been working on a series of paintings of Wabanaki tribal elders, and another series of animals from the Maine woods. The story of Rabbit had been playing in his head for months, until he remembered a little drawing of a birch tree he had made, and at last, *I Am Birch* came to life: chaos and fear as seen by a birch stump, who, against all expectations, manages to put those fears to rest.

Even a stump can be a hero.